Limonta

Hector

The Pearl

The SECRET OF THE MAGIC PEARL

Written by
ELISA SABATINELLI · IACOPO BRUNO
Illustrated by

RED COMET PRESS · BROOKLYN

The Secret of the Magic Pearl
This edition published in 2021 by Red Comet Press, LLC, Brooklyn, NY

Original title: *Mio padre è un palombaro*
Original Italian text © 2019 Elisa Sabatinelli
Illustrations © 2019 Iacopo Bruno
Art Director: Francesca Leoneschi
Graphic Project: Giovanna Ferraris/*the*World*of*DOT
Published by arrangement with Atlantyca S.p.A.
First published in Italy by RCS MediaGroup S.p.A., Milano

English adaptation © 2021 Red Comet Press, LLC
Translated by Christopher Turner
Editorial contributions: Thea Feldman
Additional translation and adaptation: Angus Yuen-Killick
Creative Director: Michael Yuen-Killick

Library of Congress Control Number: 2020952063
ISBN: 978-1-63655-006-0

21 22 23 24 25 TLF 10 9 8 7 6 5 4 3 2 1

Manufactured in China

RED COMET PRESS

RedCometPress.com

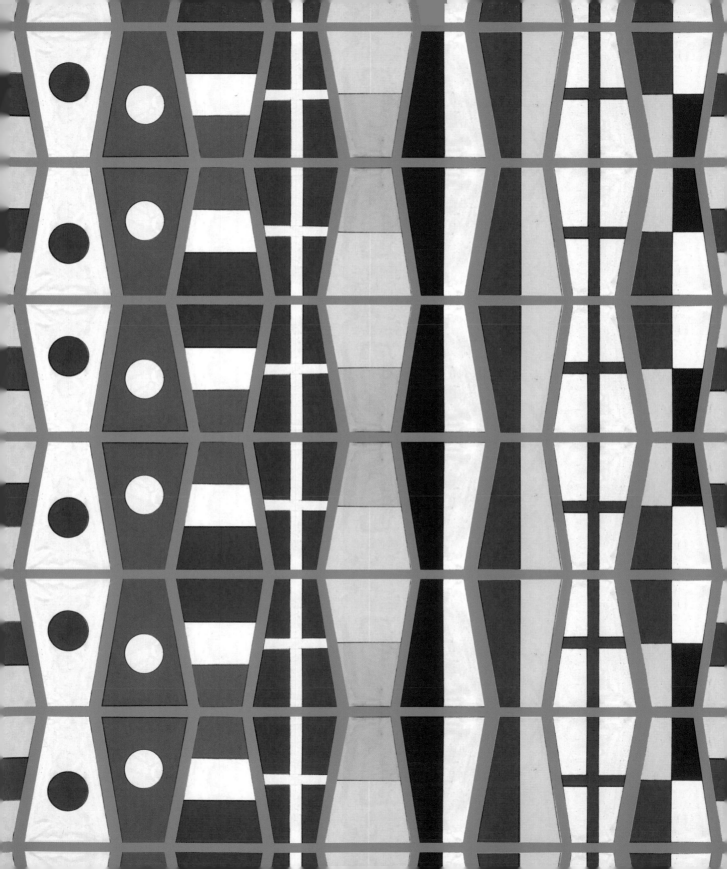

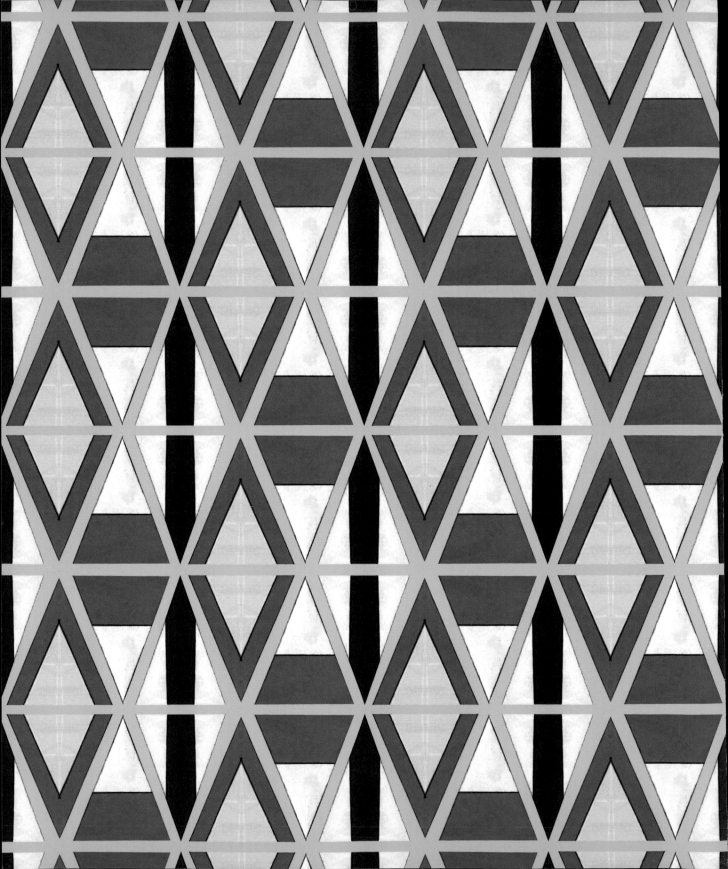

To my daughter and son, Octavia and Giovanni, whom I envy because they're children and everything seems possible to them—even this story.

Elisa, the flying fish

Dedicated to the people who helped me fall in love with the sea: Grandpa, who, in the springtime, picked me up from school and took me fishing in his boat; and Uncle Claudio, who taught me to respect the sea and steer a sailboat.

And to my wife, Francesca, who brought me to where I wanted to be: the sea!

Jacopo, the bream

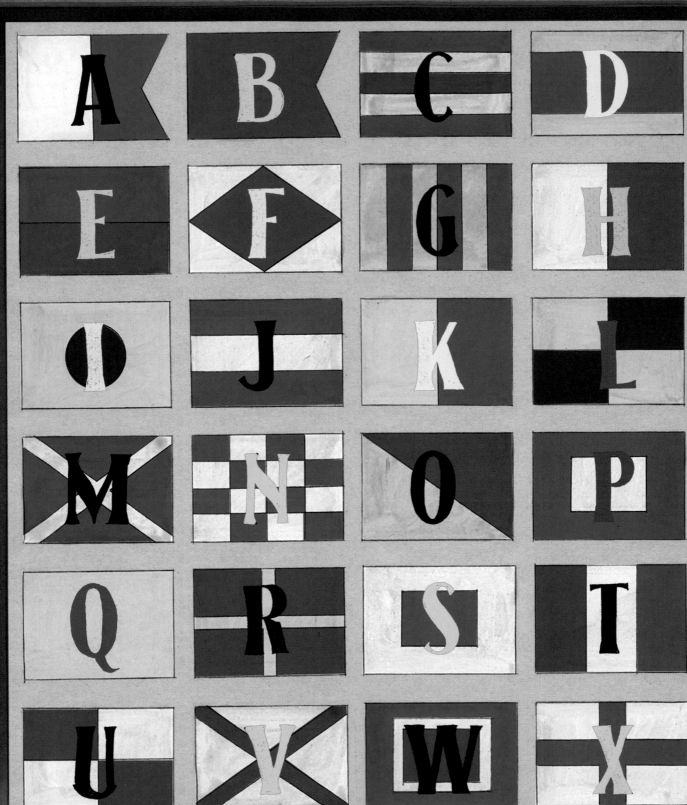

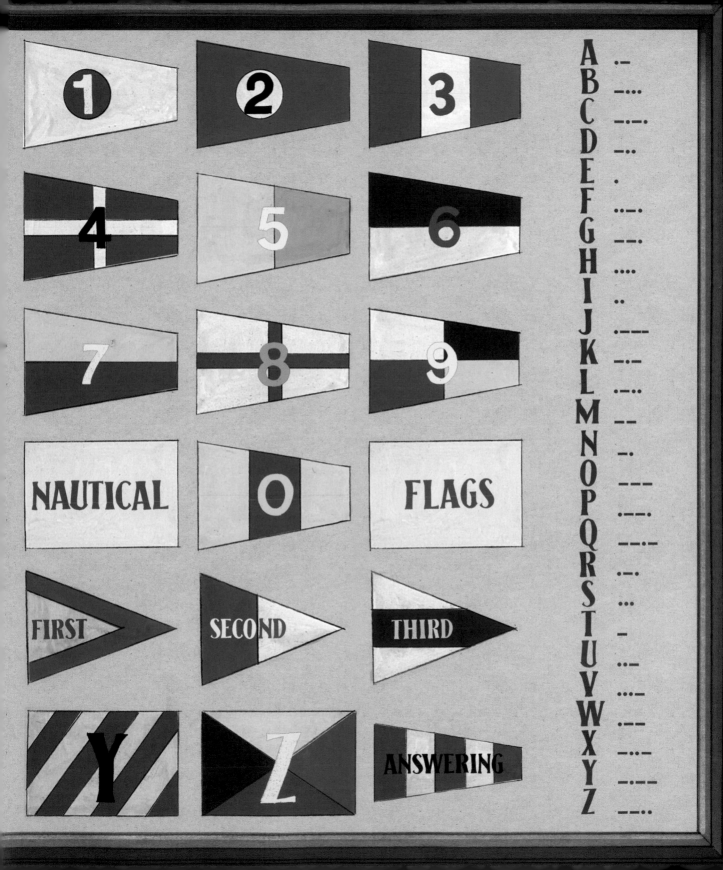

CHAPTERS

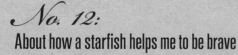

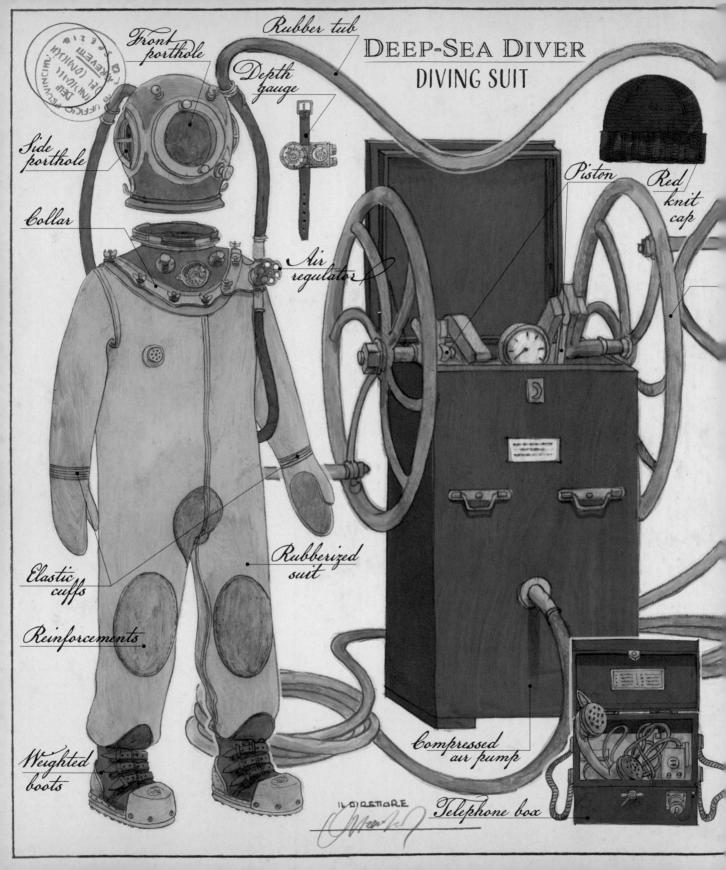

DEEP-SEA DIVER
DIVING SUIT

Front porthole

Rubber tub

Depth gauge

Side porthole

Collar

Air regulator

Piston

Red knit cap

Elastic cuffs

Reinforcements

Rubberized suit

Compressed air pump

Weighted boots

Telephone box

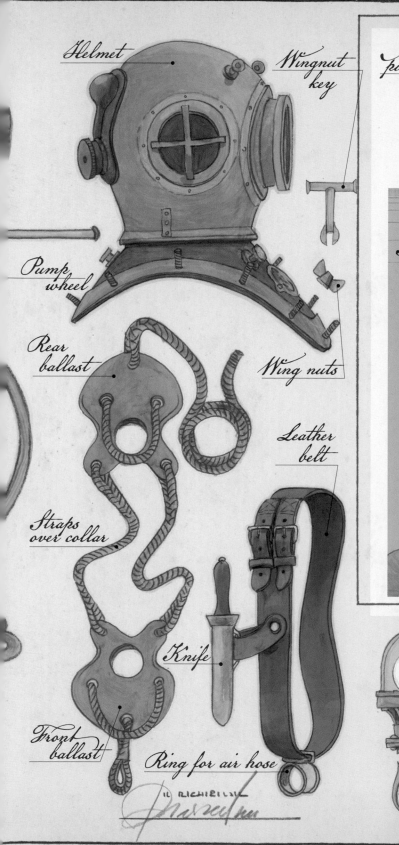

Helmet

Wingnut key

Air pump

Pump wheel

Support boat

Safety line

Rear ballast

Wing nuts

Air

Leather belt

Straps over collar

Knife

Medusa lamp

Front ballast

Ring for air hose

Weighted boots 8-10 Kg.

17 OTT

MARCA DA BOLLO LIRE 20

MARCA DA BOLLO LIRE 5

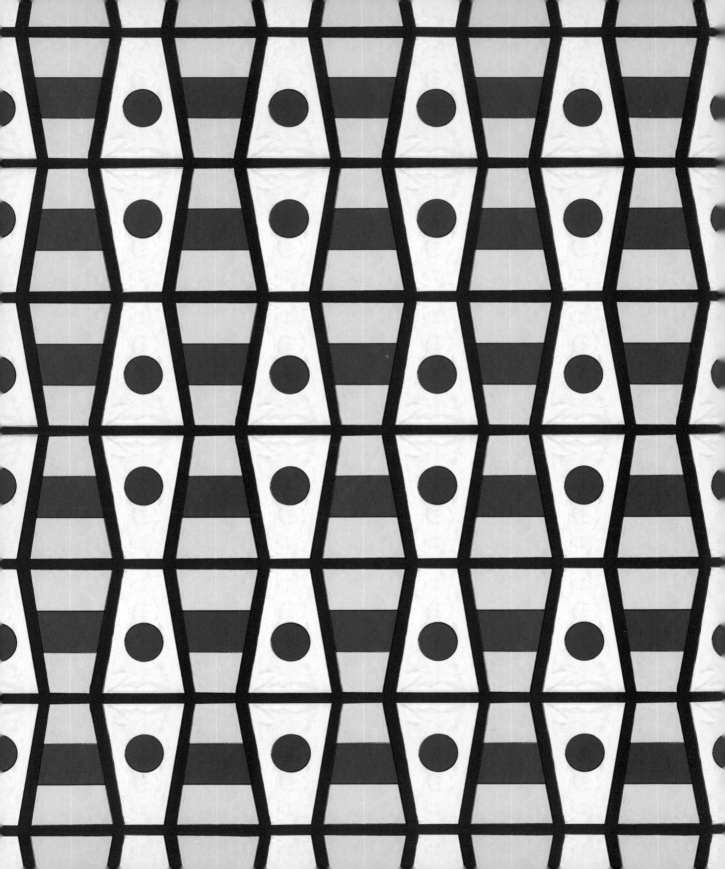

The STORY OF THE PEARL IS THE TRUEST

№ 1

My father is a deep-sea diver. His name is Hector. My name's also Hector, and, when I grow up, I want to be a deep-sea diver, too.

Dad hangs up his diving suit near the fridge in the kitchen when he comes back from dives (although he doesn't go as often as he used to) so it can drip onto the floor, which is made of marble, so it doesn't matter. Mom, who loves cooking, says the diving-suit helmet looks like a meatball.

Before we lived in this little house away from the beach, we lived with my grandparents in a big house down by the seashore. It was blue, even though the other houses there were green. Lots of ship flags waved in the

1

wind on the roof, and the windows were portholes. On the terrace, there was a big iron tank covered in pipes that looked like arms and legs. It was used to collect rainwater, but Grandpa took a bath in it once a week.

I remember there was also a basement where we kept the family's diving suits. It was amazing to see all those robots hanging there, next to nets full of things pulled out from the sea, crumpled maps stained with saltwater, rubber boots, and Torty, the tortoise with the tired eyes. There was a smell of salt and sun in the basement.

We've always been a sea family. My great-great-great-grandfather started the Marina, a diving center that, from the day it opened, was a place where divers from up and down the coast came to meet. The Marina organized underwater explorations. And it was a good place to hear stories about the sea—although no one ever knew if they were true or made up, because Grandpa loved to bring his imagination to every line.

> **IF YOU WERE BORN BY THE SEA, ITS SMELL FOLLOWS YOU FOR LIFE.**

Torty

Grandpa

The only story we were sure was true was the one about the Pearl.

The story goes that the Pearl lives on the seabed offshore from the Marina. It's a place below the blue and the waves, where the water becomes thicker and saltier. A place far from light, human voices, and even sounds. People say that it's the rarest, whitest, and purest pearl in the world. A pearl than can light up a whole room.

Even though he had lots of adventures, Grandpa never saw the Pearl. But a sailor friend of his says that her bright light guided him back home one stormy night.

Sailors call her the soul of the sea. And sailors' words are the truest, because almost all of them have had to find the courage to say painful goodbyes—often, too many times to count. Their word, like their honor, is beyond question.

I've always wanted my own deep-sea diving suit. Everyone said, "Wait till you grow up." But now that I'm older and stronger (because I'm almost eight), there's no place in the kitchen to hang a suit and no money to buy one.

When Grandpa died, the Marina went bankrupt because Amedeo Limonta came along and built a huge building next door. I've never met Amedeo Limonta but I do know the story about how he lost his honor.

Amedeo grew up in a simple family of sardiners. (That's what we call the fishermen who fish for those little fish.) Giulio, his father, was one of the most respected men in the village. Grandpa said that

Amedeo Limonta

he hardly ever spoke, but when he did, his words carried the sweet sound of the waves. One night, Giulio was taken by the sea.

Afterward, Amedeo Limonta lived alone with his mother but kept fishing for sardines.

But he wasn't happy. Some people say that the sea wind drove him mad. Others, that the salt got inside his head and made him lose his love of the ocean. Whatever happened, Amedeo and the sea became enemies. The more he cursed the waves, the angrier they grew and the more they tossed his boat. He caught fewer and fewer sardines, and the ones he did catch were smaller and smaller. The sea stopped listening to him.

Amedeo ended up with just one goal in life: to make money. So, he forgot about sardines and started fishing for bluefin tuna. And that was how he slowly lost his sailor's soul and betrayed the sea.

The Three Dimwits

During the migration, when the bluefin travel in schools, Amedeo Limonta made a huge net to catch millions of them. He then put them in big underwater cages until they grew big enough for him to sell in Japan. He made lots of money but lost the respect of the local people. And he lost the love of his wife, a beautiful woman who left one morning at dawn, swimming off toward the horizon.

When Amedeo Limonta started building Rivadoro, the big complex near the Marina, we knew what he was up to. He began organizing beginner dives and boat rides for tourists at much cheaper prices than ours, lying to people that they'd see dolphins and swordfish.

I'm sure that Limonta and his men don't know a thing about the sea because I once saw them going in the opposite direction from where the dolphins swim. I told them where to go, but they said, "Forget about it, you little shrimp!" I think it was meant to be an insult, but I like shrimp.

The Marina

Rivadoro is so clean that it makes you feel more like you're in a hospital than by the sea. Right from the start, I didn't like Amedeo Limonta, with his perfect mustache and hair that looks like it's been licked by a cow. His team is made up of three dimwits, who buzz around him like flies.

The Swimmer

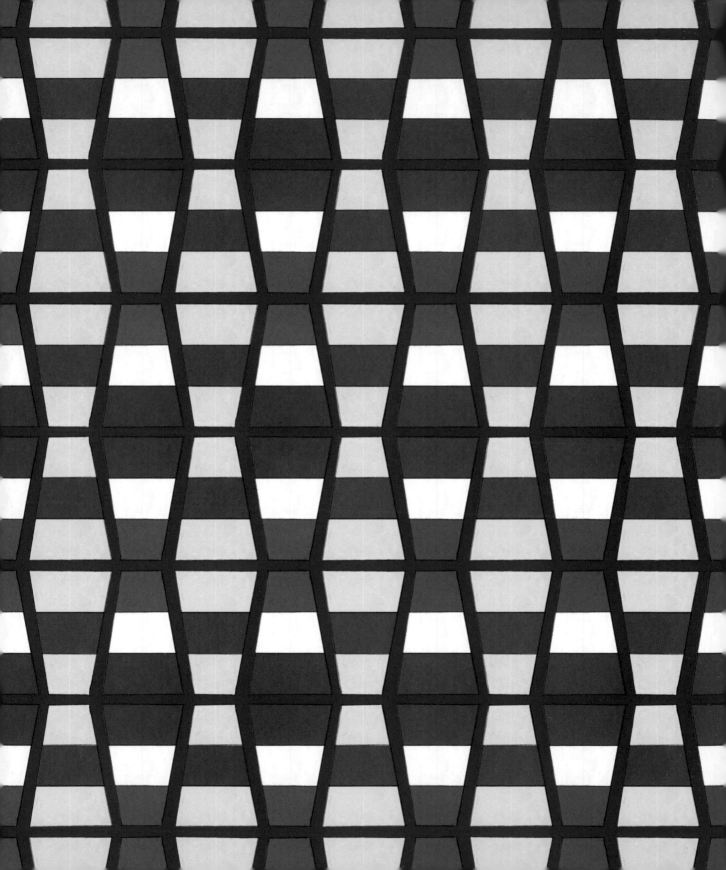

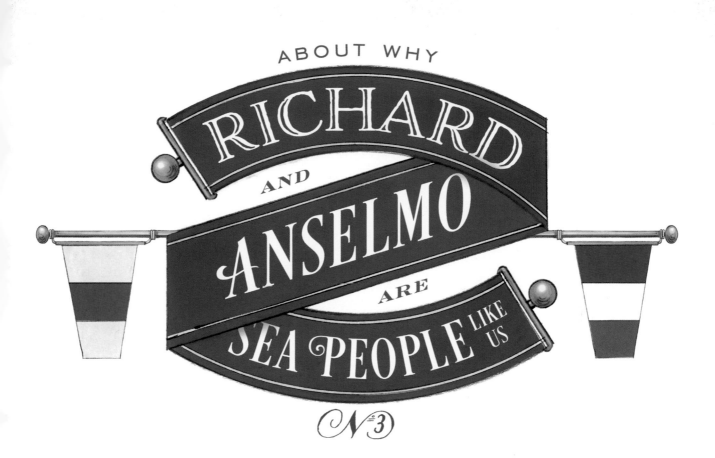

ABOUT WHY

RICHARD AND ANSELMO ARE SEA PEOPLE LIKE US

N.° 3

R ichard, a.k.a. Richard the Lionfish, is my best friend. He's the youngest of five and lives up in the hills. But he loves the sea and used to spend a lot of time with me at the Marina.

We go to the same school. He's very shy and sometimes gets bad grades because he whispers the answers to questions and the teacher can't hear what he's said. I nudge him to speak louder, but he can't. At recess, while the others swap cards, we sit on the wall at the end of the yard and swap things from the sea.

Richard and I don't understand why Amedeo Limonta built Rivadoro near the Marina when he couldn't care less about the sea. But the tourists and new people don't know

13

Richard

We don't know Anselmo very well because he never talks. But that's fine with us. He just sits and stares out to sea. That's all. The people in the village say he's mad, that his brain burned out when his house burned down, and he was the only one to survive because he put some

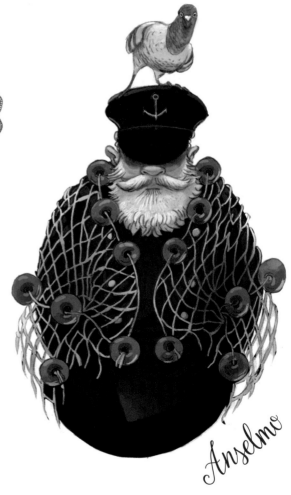

Anselmo

anything about his bad past. So, while Rivadoro gets more and more customers, the only person who goes to the Marina now is Anselmo, who sits on the steps in front of the locked front door and listens to the waves.

of the fire out with the aquarium he had in his bedroom and then escaped.

I understand Anselmo. And if he doesn't want to talk, we don't mind. We leave him in peace. He wears a fishing net like a cape, and when you see him from a distance, sitting by the sea, he looks like an ancient statue.

Dad tried everything to keep the Marina open. A few months before it closed, he started handing out a flyer that he made and I photocopied at school. And it was beautiful, with lots of different colors and the words

"Come and discover the incredible surprises of the sea!"

There were pictures of shells, coral, and fish as colorful as rainbows. But the school photocopier only did black and white, so the flyers came out gray and dead-looking, like advertisements for a cave.

When people stopped coming to the marina, my father decided to close it.

We then moved to the tiny house where we live now. The only things we brought from the Marina were Dad's diving suit and the map that Grandpa had used to mark all the places he'd been at sea. Before I go to sleep at night, I stare at the bare walls of my new room and repeat to myself, "One day I'll go to all those places, too!"

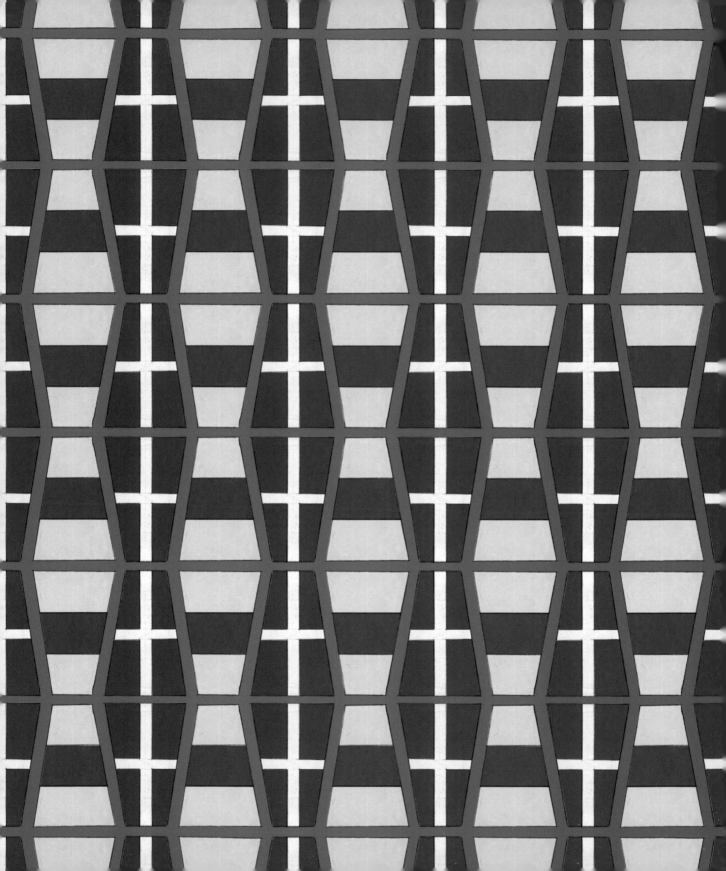

The BAD GUY

DREAMS

of CAPTURING

THE

PEARL

Nº 4

My father now works at the tourist information office in the village, where his job is to describe our local attractions to visitors. But he doesn't like being stuck inside a building, in his street clothes, away from the sea. He does it because he has to, because he wants to take Mom and me on a vacation.

Dad still dreams of going back to the sea. He's not scared of sharks, jellyfish, or typhoons. He's never said no to the sea. He's a true diver, one of those people who puts on his deep-sea diving suit and walks on the seabed in search of ancient things to bring back to the surface. The only thing that scares him is not finding more shipwrecks and,

La MARINA

therefore, not having any more stories to tell.

The other day, the three of us—Mom, Dad, and I—went for a swim in front of the Marina. It was very sad to see it all shut up with padlocks, planks of wood nailed over the windows, and seagulls circling overhead. At Rivadoro next door, tourists were lining up for a sightseeing cruise.

Dad didn't even open the Marina door. You should have seen his face: it was sadder than sad.

He said, "Let's go. There's no place here for us anymore."

Where our life, our family, and our dreams had been, Amedeo Limonta has built a huge tourist attraction that's more in demand than the Marina ever was. A few days ago, they started offering tourists sponge-diving trips to make even more money. They have radar and all kinds of modern equipment.

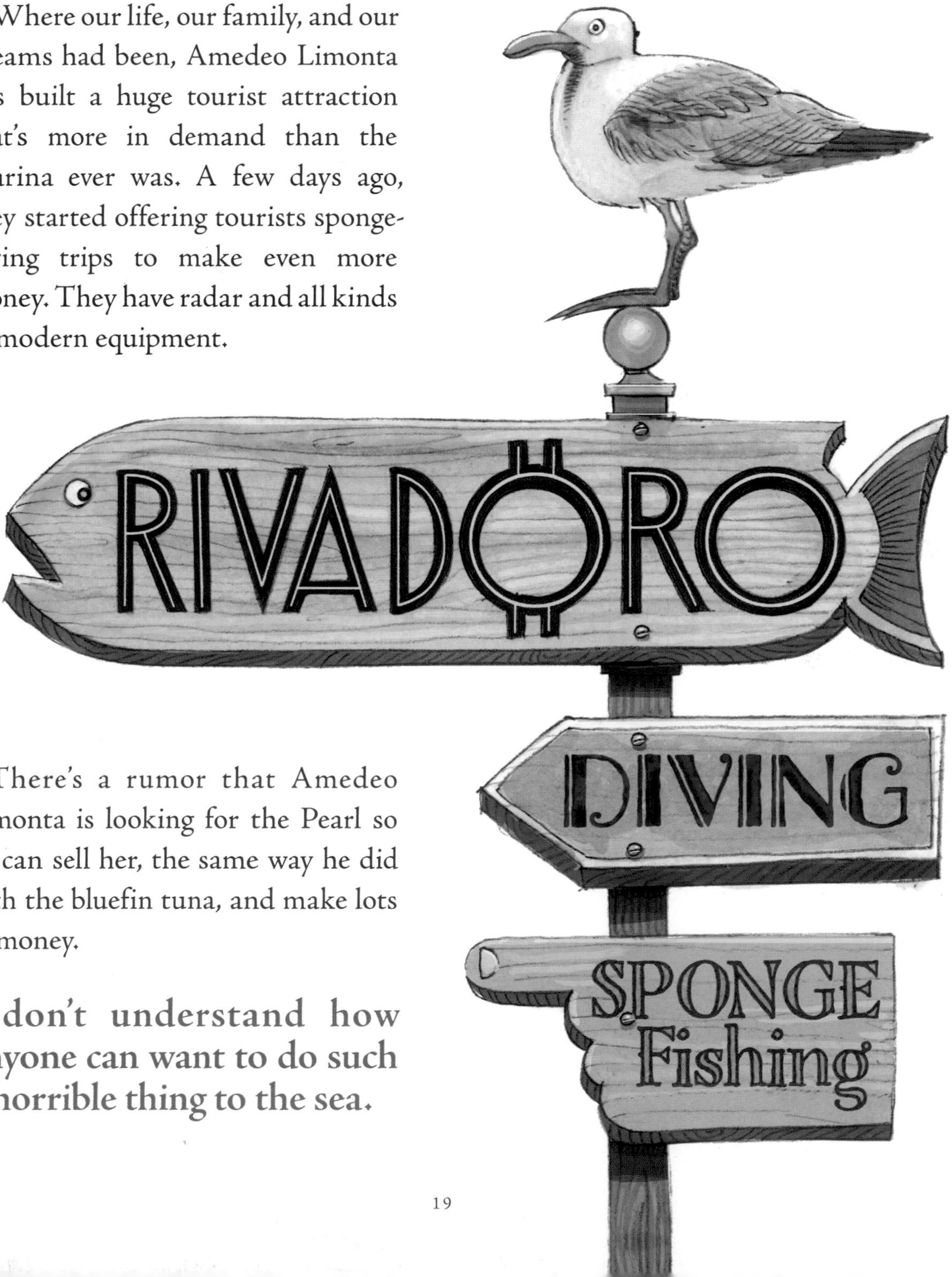

There's a rumor that Amedeo Limonta is looking for the Pearl so he can sell her, the same way he did with the bluefin tuna, and make lots of money.

I don't understand how anyone can want to do such a horrible thing to the sea.

RIVADORO

DIVING

SPONGE Fishing

Nº 5

Carlotta, Amedeo Limonta's daughter, is my age and wears pearl necklaces and pearl bracelets to school. Her father even calls her "my little pearl." She always has a high ponytail, which she pulls so tight that she looks like a tropical fish, with her eyes on either side of her head. She never smiles or talks much and so always sits by herself at recess. Most people think she's just stuck up because her father is so rich. But I think she may be sad because her mother left a long time ago, when Amedeo Limonta stopped believing in the sea.

The other girls at school are all the daughters of divers or fishmongers.

Carlotta

They play at selling pretend sole and cod. Carlotta never joins in.

Richard thinks she may be shy, like him. He fell in love with her on the first day of school, when Carlotta asked him in her very low but sweet voice, "Can you hear the school bell properly from the schoolyard?"

The school bell is an old maritime ship's bell and it goes off at midday to let you know that it's almost time to go home. It's the only part of school that Richard likes. I prefer the sound of the foghorn, though, which they use at sea to guide sailors back to land.

Carlotta's question made my friend as soft as overboiled fish, because it was the first time a girl had paid any attention to him.

Richard the Lionfish asked me for advice on how to make her like him. "Give her a box of the things we collect from the sea!" I suggested. He did, but Carlotta just looked at the box and then at Richard and didn't say anything. That really upset Richard, and since then, he keeps the box in his pocket just in case, one day, Limonta's daughter will accept it.

I'm sorry that my friend is sad and I feel a little guilty, too. But when I told mom about it, she said I shouldn't.

"This Carlotta sounds very rude to me," she said. I already knew she'd say that. There are two things Mom always harps on about: manners and education.

And she's totally obsessed with education. She reads a lot, and a lot of the things I know about the sea, I learned from her. "Heads need to be filled up! But not with air like balloons! You need to study and learn as many things as you can. But it's even more important to think with your heart. Anyone who puts on a diving suit must have the brains to navigate the sea and the

heart to love it. That's the only way it will reveal itself to you in all its beauty."

I want to be a deep-sea diver more than anything, and I never forget her words. I dream of sailing the sea, going down to the seabed, walking among treasures from the past . . . In my room, I've got twenty-three posters and fifty-four photographs of Jacques Cousteau, who was like one of the musketeers of the sea.

Dad and he are my heroes.

Jacques-Yves Cousteau

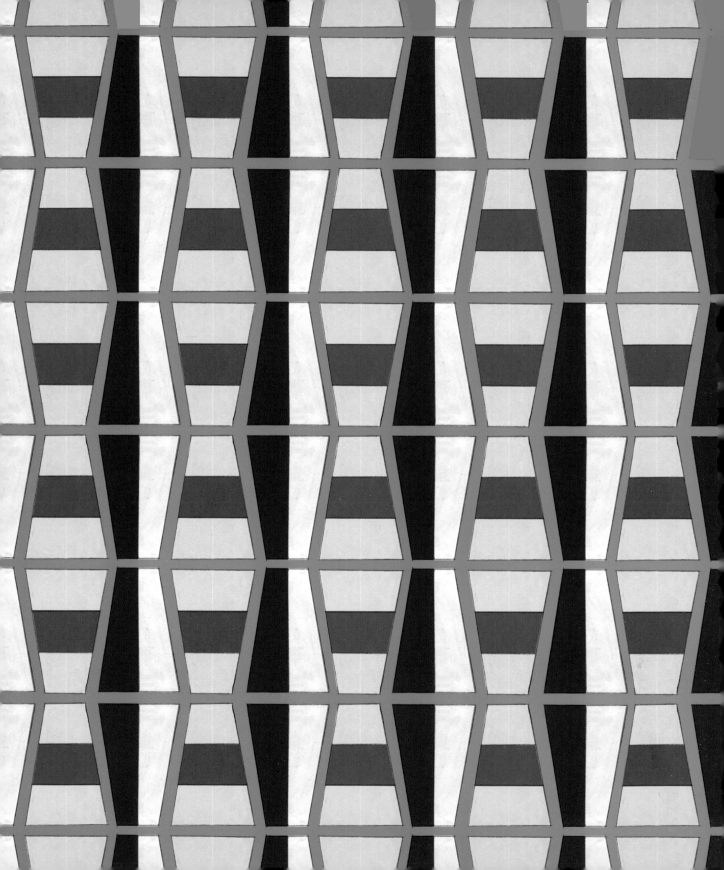

ABOUT WHY TODAY *is* MY BEST BIRTHDAY EVER

N⁰ 6

Today is my birthday. I'm turning eight. Mom has made a big orange cake in the shape of a diving suit with lots of cream. It's beautiful, and I'm almost sorry to eat it. I'd like to keep it in the basement with the family diving suits!

After I blow out the candles, Dad finally says the words that I've always dreamed of hearing, "Hector, now that you're big, next Sunday we'll walk on the seabed together. But you'll have to borrow a diving suit from one of your friends . . ." I jump up and touch the ceiling, then give Dad and Mom big hugs.

"I'm sorry we can't give you your own new diving suit," Mom says in a sad voice.

Danny Flippers

I give her a big smile and cry, "I don't care about getting a new one!" And I mean it. "Jacques Cousteau didn't have much when he started out: just a blue suit, a red hat, and some flippers."

Dad always says that the most important thing you need to be an explorer is imagination. To be on the crew of Jacques Cousteau's *Calypso*, all you needed was a red hat. And I had one! So, with my hat, and a lot of imagination, I went straight to Daniel's house. Daniel who everyone calls Danny Flippers, is a few years older than me and has hair as curly as the breakers. But it turns out that he doesn't have a suit. He doesn't like diving, just swimming. With flippers, of course.

So I run to Maria's house. Her nickname is Seahorse because she can float no matter what. But my head's too big for her helmet. Then I go to David the Flying Squid's, Ten Tentacles Fred's, and Richard's, but none of them have a diving suit that fits me.

So I go home and start searching in the attic, where Mom keeps all the things we don't use anymore but doesn't want to throw out because "they're memories" and "memories tell us about ourselves, who we've

Maria Seahorse

David the Flying Squid

been, and where we came from, even when we're grown-up and think we know everything."

I get lucky and find some orange waterproof overalls that Dad wore when he was little and cleaned the beach with Grandpa every morning. They're great! All shiny with a blue zipper, the color of the sea, and *MARINA* written on the back. I get a marker, change the last *A* to an *E* and add the word *CAPTAIN*, so it reads *CAPTAIN MARINE*. Before putting it on, I put on the woolen vest my father made me, a pair of Mom's socks, and Grandpa's scarf, so that

not so much as a single chill will get in while I'm in the water.

I keep looking, and, inside a rusty bicycle's basket, I find a pair of leather boots that look so old they make me think they'd be good for diving. I get two pieces of the iron that Grandpa used to use to mend the tank and glue them to the soles.

Now all I have to think of is my head. After looking through the piles of stuff in all the trunks and boxes, I decide to try the Marina.

Ten Tentacles Fred

I sneak inside. Down in the basement, I find a ruined old diving suit, covered in dog chew marks and bits of coral. The helmet isn't really my size, but that isn't going to stop me. And there are a few bolts missing, but I replace them with screws.

It's now Sunday morning and I'm ready to dive!

I have tomatoes on toast for breakfast. I put on my diving suit and Mom takes a photo of me near the fridge and next to Dad's diving suit. Before she lets me go, she gives me a hug and says, "Be careful! Keep your eyes wide open. You're going to see marvelous things down there! Break a leg!" She always says this thing about breaking a leg. I've got no idea what it means.

My heart's pounding as I walk down the road to the sea, counting the steps as I go. Dad's looking out at the horizon. You can smell saltwater in the air.

ABOUT WHY SINKING IN THE SEA IS LIKE WALKING ON THE MOON

N.º 7

Here we are! The sea is calm and flat, sparkling and very salty. Anselmo is getting ready to go out in his boat. He gives us a quick nod, which in his wordless language means, "Do you want me to take you out?"

"Thanks, Anselmo. Could you, please? Today's a special day. It's Hector's first dive!" Anselmo's hard gaze melts away, and he hugs me in a salty embrace.

Our friend takes us out to where the water is darker. There are other boats out here. Some people are fishing and others are swimming. We're the only divers.

Dad goes down first. His diving suit disappears under the water as he sinks down, down, and farther

31

Coral

down. I follow him straight away.

The moment I'm in the water, I feel a unique silence—as if someone has closed off the world with a stopper. How much water is in the sea? I'd love to measure it. I sink down until I touch the bottom. It's like the ground of our world, but walking down there is like being on another planet. There's nothing but silence, a calm that makes me think of Sunday mornings. It's like being on the Moon. Up and down don't really matter. Either way, I'm just as far from planet Earth.

The only thing we do to disturb that peace is to throw up a cloud of fine sand with each step we take. But we walk slowly. We're in no hurry. A squid darts by and seems to smile at me. As we pass by, I see coral swaying and seaweed bending to-and-fro. I'm happy. I look at my father, who gives me a wave and signals me to go on ahead.

Now I'm the one leading the expedition. The rocks seem to move back as I go forward, as if they're opening a passage

for me. I feel protected under the silent, peaceful water.

I close my eyes like Grandpa used to, who'd let himself be rocked like a baby by the currents because under the water he was a child again. He always said to me, "I'm only old on land, not in the sea. You never age down there. You remain forever as light as you were when you were little."

After a while, I open my eyes again, because seeing those wonderful things is too special to miss. There's a hermit crab's house with the crab's

Hermit Crab

orange legs poking out the bottom, thin red seaweed like fans, and silver fish darting here and there. Long and thin with crooked teeth, a school of barracuda swims by. And then more colorful fish and shells and rocks and hairy sponges.

My father points to a school of mullet a short distance away, and I hope that a bluefish won't come along and eat them all. I'd never want to meet one of them with their sharp teeth like traps! I get distracted for a moment and don't see the mullet again.

The blue down here doesn't exist anywhere else. It's not sea-blue or midnight-blue, like people think. It has its own special light—a kind of floating gold dust that makes it unique; it almost glitters.

A friend of grandpa's has tried to describe this color to me many times, but he always ends up saying, "It only exists in dreams."

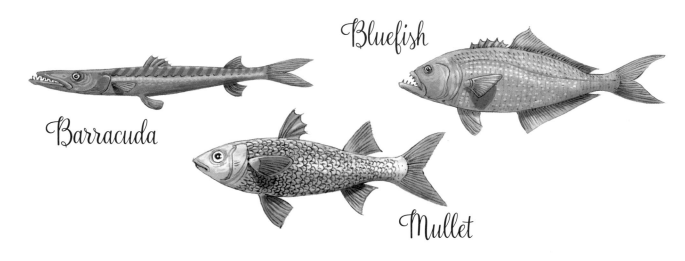

Bluefish

Barracuda

Mullet

There's an ancient statue ahead of us. It looks like a dream, too. My mother told me its story once. The statue has been here for a long, long time. It's of a very tall man in a tunic that goes down to his feet and his arms are raised toward the sky. He's the protector of sailors, and there's a tradition for people to visit him on their first dive. Tiny fish swim all around him, creating a spiral of flowers. Some green seaweed drops off one of his arms. I watch it as it settles down to the bottom.

Just then I notice a light shining between the statue's ankles. I go closer, and the light flashes on and off, as if it's calling to me.

There, almost completely buried by sand, I find her. I find the Pearl! I brush the sand off her and a white glow shines all around us. I look into Dad's eyes through the glass of his helmet. He's staring and waving his hands like a madman. Then he does a few somersaults. He's very happy! He keeps smiling as I rub the Pearl. Her energy enters my body with a force like being hit by a wave. She's wonderful, and she doesn't seem at all frightened by us since she's not trying to bury herself back under the sand.

The impulse to show her to Mom is too strong to resist. So I gently scoop her up between my hands.

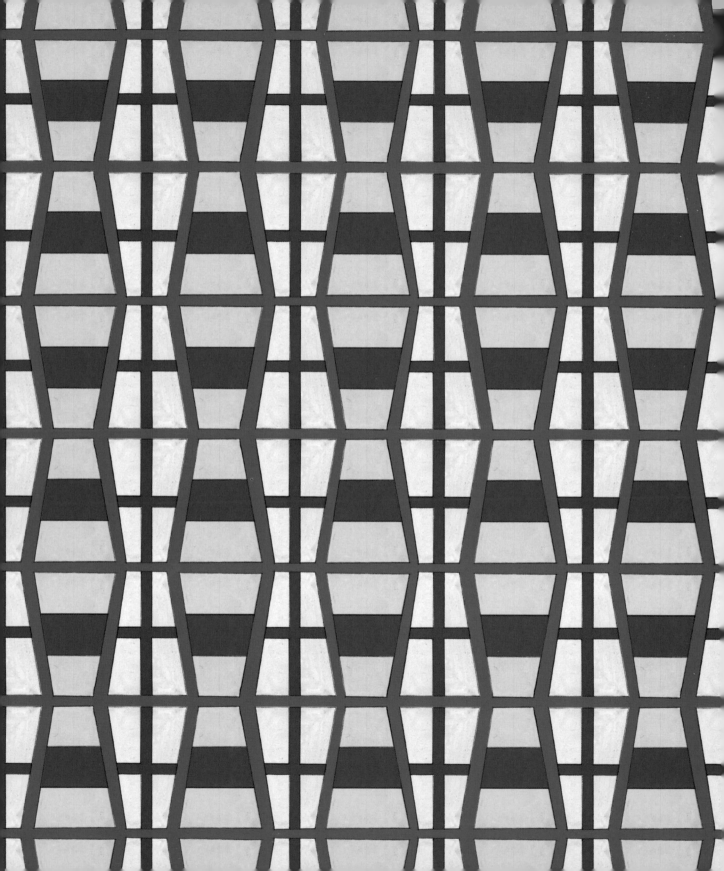

BAD GUYS

ARE

SOMETIMES

GOOD

(OR SEEM TO BE)

N⁸

The next day, the newspaper headlines are all about me: "Captain Marine discovers the secret of the sea!" "Eight-year-old boy finds the Pearl!" "Captain Marine and the Pearl!"

It was Mom who phoned Ludovica Martinelli, a journalist with our local newspaper and our next-door neighbor back at the Marina.

According to Mom and Dad, good news should be shared. So, the good news was soon on the TV and radio and in the newspapers.

On TV you can see the journalists getting wet as they do their reports too close to the breakers on the beach. They talk about the "golden beach." My parents and I sit in the living room watching and reading all these things, while the Pearl sits on the bottom of a green bottle of mineral water.

The phone rings, and I answer. It's a journalist with a high-pitched voice. "Hi there, Captain Marine!" he says. "Did you know that this pearl you found is worth a lot of money?" Then, without giving me time to answer, he asks, "What do you want to do when you grow up?" I think about it. I look around. I'm so confused and so happy that nothing makes sense,

and I can't think of an answer.

Dad's smoking a pipe. He hasn't smoked since Grandpa died. A decision has to be made: What should we do with the Pearl?

Like every time we need to make a decision, Mom is the one who eventually does it: we have to take the Pearl back to the sea. But before doing that, she says, we should put it on display so that other people can admire it, too. Mom always says we should share beautiful things.

I suggest that we dedicate a whole room of our house—mine—to the Pearl, like a museum. It's no big deal for me to sleep on the couch.

The first day is a big success: hundreds of people line up to see the Pearl, which shines with a glow that takes everyone's breath away. No one needs a flash to take a photo: the Pearl shines with a light of her own. I've left all my posters up in my room so people can look at them, too, because they're so good.

At school, the kids all look at me with their eyes full of admiration. I'm not Hector anymore but Captain Marine. Everyone wants to know how I found it. And they all look so riveted that I even tell one kid that I fought a shark to get it. But it's a lie. Even Carlotta, who always spends recess by herself, seems to be interested in me because of the Pearl, and she sticks to me like

an anemone to a rock. She is very annoying, because she waits for me every morning on the steps outside the school, so we always end up going into class together, even though she never says a word. Richard pretends to look out the window, but I know he's only doing that so he doesn't have to look at us. (All you can see out our classroom window is the restrooms, and they're really not worth looking at.)

I'm not too sure if Carlotta's father, Amedeo Limonta, would be happy with her waiting for me like that, because the news that I'd found the Pearl made him furious. He went on all the TV stations, screaming horrible things about my father and me. He said that the part of the sea where I found the Pearl belongs to him and therefore the Pearl is his as well. And things like that. He's so

SOMETIMES PEOPLE BECOME FAMOUS FOR SOMETHING THAT SEEMS TOTALLY NORMAL TO THEM.

angry, with his hair all messy, pacing up and down on the beach, sending up a dust cloud of sand. But his anger doesn't stop people from wanting to see the Pearl, and more and more people are coming every day, even from other towns.

What surprises us more than the people, though, is Amedeo Limonta himself. A few days after his TV appearance he shows up at our house with his men. As if that isn't strange enough, he starts being very kind to my mother and keeps saying how lovely she is. Dad tries to distract them, asking if they want tea, coffee, juice, a cold drink, a sparkling water, a still water, an iced water … Limonta then compliments me and everything else in the house. I don't believe anything he says, but he doesn't stop me from feeling happy.

Carlotta is here, too, and Mom makes us anchovy and tomato sandwiches to eat out on the terrace, while Amedeo Limonta and his men go into my room to see the Pearl. I don't want to spend time with Carlotta, but Mom says I have to because of manners.

"Did you like the box Richard gave you?" I ask, just so I don't have to sit there like a stunned mullet with nothing to say.

For a long minute, Carlotta just looks at me with her big fish eyes. Finally, she looks down and starts to speak.

"Yes," she says so quietly, I have to lean forward to hear her. "But I was so surprised by the gift that I couldn't talk! And I feel bad, because I think I hurt his feelings, and he took it back. And now I don't know what to say to him." Then she looks up at me and her eyes get wide in embarrassment at what she has just told me. Then she jumps up and runs off to see the Pearl.

So Richard *was* right. Carlotta *is* shy! I am going to have to help these two become friends!

Over the next few days, there is a steady stream of visitors to see the Pearl, including several who recount their own adventures in searching for it. One bearded sailor seems so overcome with emotion, we give him a few minutes alone with the Pearl. From the living room, we hear him mutter with excitement, "My little pearl, my little pearl."

Every evening, I, too, sit down alone with the Pearl. She is so beautiful.

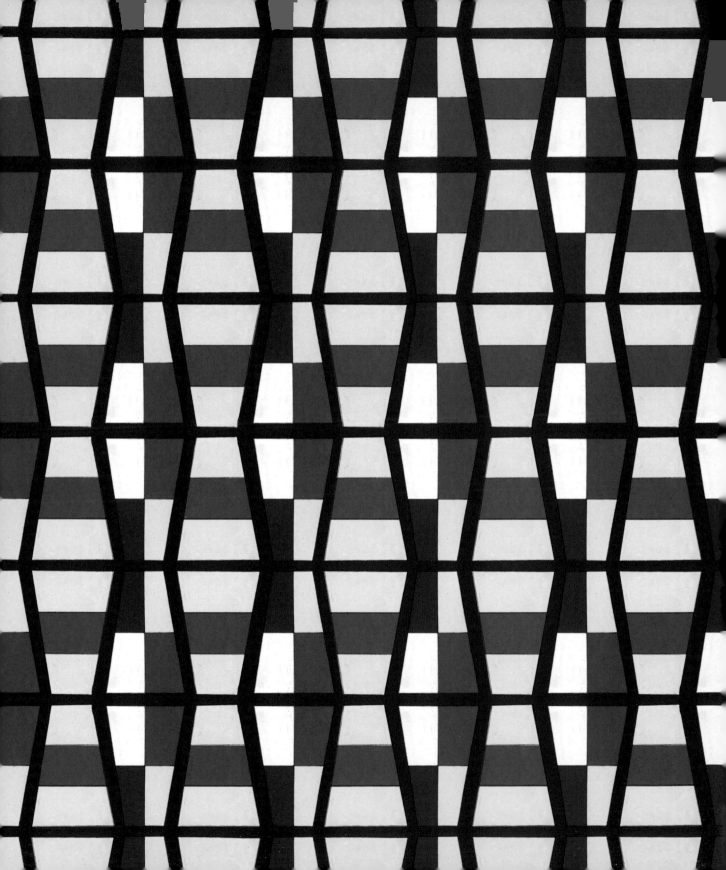

Over the next few days, I concentrate on my schoolwork, so I don't have to listen to Mom grumbling. Dad's feeling enthusiastic again, though. The discovery of the Pearl has given him a new confidence, and at lunch and dinner he talks about opening the Marina again.

Dad's enthusiasm gives him good ideas, but, for some reason, it also seems to be hurting the Pearl. I notice that she's not shining the way she used to. Her light is much weaker, even dim. Other people notice it, too, and rumors start spreading at school. Rumors like, "The whole thing was made up!" and "It's not the real Pearl! It's a fake!" and even "Captain Marine planned the whole thing to trick us!"

The rumors get worse every day. The other kids stop asking me questions. Richard is the only one who still believes me. He never doubts me.

At home, I overhear Mom and Dad arguing. Someone at the tourist information office called Dad a liar. This is too much! I have to do something.

I try to imagine what the Pearl is feeling. Then it occurs to me that even though I like going to new places, after a while I always start to miss Mom and Dad.

The Pearl is homesick!

I decide that I have to take her back to the sea. But to do it, I'm going to have to come up with a plan, because they say that unscrupulous, money-hungry men are keeping watch over the beach day and night, waiting for me to take it back to where I found it.

In the meantime, I collect fresh seaweed, pebbles, pieces of rock, sand from the seabed, and driftwood from the shore. I then make an altar with all those things from her world. I'm sure that, in a few days, the Pearl will start to feel better.

But things don't work out that way. I do my best to make her happy, but the Pearl's light eventually goes out and she shows no sign of getting better. It's as if her magic has gone, and I don't know the spell to bring it back.

The only good news I have is that I've finally gotten Richard and Carlotta to start talking to one another, and they are even planning to go out together in Richard's boat! That *is* big news, but not enough to take my mind off the Pearl.

One day, I get home from school feeling very tired and go straight to bed. My dreams are tinged with black.

They're dark and deep, and I find myself deep under the sea. It's so cold and so, so dark down there. I can't even see my own shadow. I swim because there's nothing else I can do. Every so often, something brushes against my belly, between my feet, behind my neck. But it only lasts a fraction of a second. Like cold chills. I soon start to feel tired and, just as I'm giving in to it, Grandpa appears. He looks worried. He says, "If you treat the sea well, it will take care of you."

I wake up with a start and out of breath. I've finally understood that the only way to show the sea that I love it is to forget about the bad guys on the beach and take the Pearl back right away. The sea wants its soul back, and I have to return it—along with the driftwood, the sand, and the rocks—to the world where she belongs, in the same way as I belong to the earth or a cloud to the sky.

If you treat the sea well...

...it will take care of you.

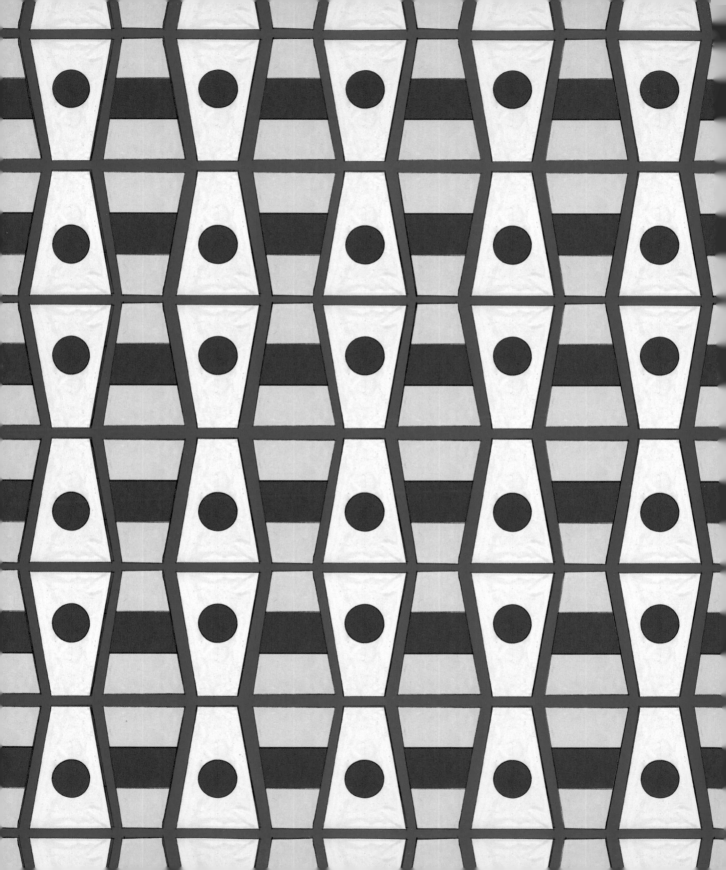

I FEEL SAD, LONELY, AND SNIFFLY

Nº 10

I wait for dawn to come, put on my diving suit, and take the Pearl. Dad's asleep in the armchair. I sneak out the front door. I'm planning to be back home before everyone gets up and I'll explain everything then.

The road is still full of the shadows of houses and trees. Their shapes blend with mine, and my shadow in the diving suit looks like an astronaut walking on the moon.

Just then, I notice that the ground is gradually being covered with white dots. I look up and see that it's starting to rain. I soon realize that the Pearl is changing color. The rain seems to be washing paint off her, and she's turning into a transparent glass ball. I hold her up to look at her more closely. I can see right through her to the Marina, where Anselmo is sitting on the steps like always. There isn't a trace of the notorious pearl hunters.

I go and sit down next to Anselmo, feeling unhappy. I'm wearing the diving suit, the sea is in front of me, but in my hand is nothing but a glass ball.

"The storm is coming."

So, he does speak! Hearing Anselmo's voice makes me smile for an instant. This is the first time I've heard him say a whole sentence! In all these years, I've only ever heard him grunt a yes or no. "It's just a drop of rain," I point out.

"Look at that waterspout," he says, pointing out to sea.

"What does it mean?"

"This isn't a normal storm. The sea is joining the sky. Something is wrong. They want to tell us about something that we can't control."

Just then, a flock of seagulls flies low over the water, moving in a spiraling, frenetic pattern. They're frightened, too. They can't fly any higher because of the north-easterly wind that's announcing the storm's arrival.

"The sea doesn't forgive . . ." The words come out of my mouth without me realizing it.

In the distance, on the other side of the Marina, I see Richard setting out in his boat with Carlotta. Oh, no! They're going out in the boat *today*, of all days?!

I have to warn them before it's too late. I start waving my arms "Come back!" I yell with all my breath.

But he makes a heart shape with his hands and doesn't hear me. I scream even louder, but my voice gets lost in the waves. Richard is suddenly forced to concentrate on rowing, while, on shore, where I am, big drops of rain turn the sand into a dark carpet.

Yes, the storm is coming.

And my best friend is out in the choppy sea in a boat with Carlotta.

I don't know what to do and run back and forth. I'm angry at the sea. I don't understand it anymore. I yell, cry salty tears, clench my fists, and sniff. I feel so alone. The kids at school are right: the Pearl is a fake.

With me stuck in my own thoughts, Anselmo gets up to leave. Before going, though, he says something that sounds a lot like one of Mom's pearls of wisdom, "The Pearl never loses her shine. Not even if she's far from the sea. In fact, the farther from the sea she is, the more she shines as she tries to get back home."

I'm confused. I think back over the days when all those people came to see her . . . There were so many, including that bearded sailor who was alone with the Pearl and kept muttering, "My little pearl!" not realizing we could hear him. That phrase . . . I realize now that it sounds so familiar the way he said it . . . Was that really a sailor, or was it someone in disguise who wanted the Pearl for himself?

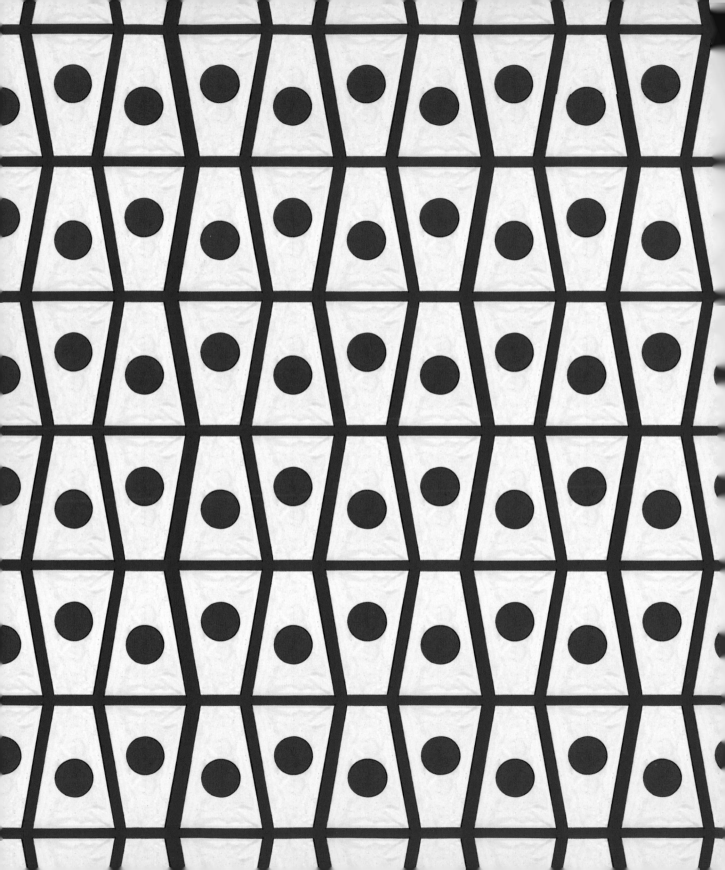

ABOUT WHY

The STORM Is Raging
AND
THERE'S
NO TIME
to LOSE
Nº 11

With the sea growing rougher and rougher and thunder rumbling in the distance, I'm scared that something awful is going to happen to Richard and Carlotta. That makes me act quickly. There's no time to lose.

I pound on Rivadoro's front door. Amedeo Limonta opens, looking very annoyed. With all this wind, of course sand blows inside. I dive inside and tell him that Richard and Carlotta are out in the storm. On a boat. Alone. Then I say, "And this isn't a normal storm!"

"All storms are the same. And your friend knows how to handle a boat. I know him."

"No. This storm won't go away by itself."

"All storms blow over sooner or later."

"The only way to stop this one is to take the Pearl back to the sea."

"And what's that got to do with me?"

"The Pearl is here. You stole her from my house. You came to my house a second time, disguised as a sailor, and were alone with her." I look him right in the eye, the way you do when you're telling the truth.

He looks away. The windows rattle heavily. Outside, a sandy whirlwind has formed, picking up everything in its path. Angry with white foam, the sea looks like a mad dog frothing at the mouth. Lightning splits the sky like a zipper.

"We made this storm and now we have to appease it, or Carlotta and Richard will be swallowed up by the waves." I'm frantic, and my palms are sweating.

With the veins bulging on his neck, Amedeo Limonta grabs me by the throat and shouts, "I've waited forever to own the Pearl!

I want to take back my fisherman's soul!"

"The Pearl doesn't belong to you," I whisper. "It belongs to the sea." I want to tell him that he needs to feel the sea in his heart, to feel waves crashing against his chest, his skin rough from the sun, and his nails dirty with fish scales. But I don't dare: he's so much taller, bigger, and crueler than me.

The Pearl is the sea. Taking her back to the seabed is what a real fisherman would do.

Limonta orders one of his dimwits to go out and get his daughter. But there are no motorboats, only a rowboat, and the man doesn't know how to row. "You stupid, incompetent blobfish!" Limonta yells.

"I know how to use a rowboat and I have my diving suit," I say. "But you'll have to come with me because I can't dive alone. I need your help." Limonta gazes out the window for a while and finally says, "Let's go get my *real* little pearl."

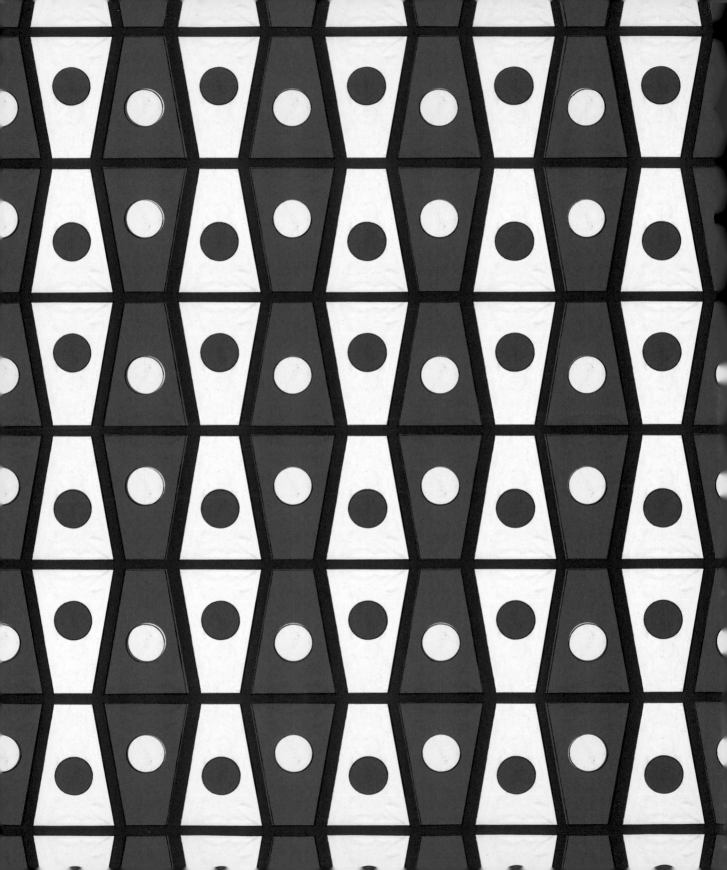

Stepping outside, the storm swallows us up. My diving suit protects me from the sand and the wind, but Amedeo Limonta's hair and mustache blow every which way. The Pearl is safe, though, protected under his jacket.

The waves are as high as mountains, and when we start rowing, the black rain clouds don't let as much as a ray of sunshine through, even though the sun has been up for some time now. The Pearl gives us light.

Out at sea, the sky and water are black and angry. The waves swell up and down in valleys and peaks, while our boat barely stays afloat. Limonta is terrified. And so am I. So I close my eyes and imagine the calm sea on a sunny day with Grandpa—that's

the sea I know and want to see again. When I open my eyes again, I spot a small boat with two even smaller figures on board as it appears and disappears between the waves as they open and close like stage curtains.

I try to reassure Limonta. "Everything will be okay." He's angry, though. As angry as the black sea raging all around us. Something wet sprays me, and I have no idea if it's rain, seawater, or saliva. He speaks so fast that I can't understand him. And the thunder is so loud, I can't hear him, either. He grabs me by the shoulders, shakes me, and babbles something. He's very afraid.

I point to his daughter's boat and scream as loud as I can, "Give me the Pearl! I have to take her home or the sea will get even angrier!"

Limonta hesitates for a moment.

But after a massive wave almost overturns us, he desperately hands me the Pearl. "Dive!"

I sink through the water with the Pearl in my hand. But going down is difficult. I can't stabilize. I try to move in one direction, but the currents toss me back. Luckily, a starfish comes to show me the way. It looks familiar to me. . . . I follow it and finally make it to the bottom. I lay the Pearl down among some rocks.

> "TO OVERCOME FEAR," GRANDPA ALWAYS SAID, "THINK ABOUT AFTERWARDS OR TOMORROW, AND BE BRAVE."

She's now back home and can again flood the sea with the same energy that lit up my room. A cone of white light shines out from among the rocks and, magically, the water stops churning. Calm slowly returns.

It feels good down here now! Even though I would love to stay, I go back to the surface. Richard and Carlotta are waiting for me. And so are Mom and Dad, school, games, and Sundays by the sea. They're all so special.

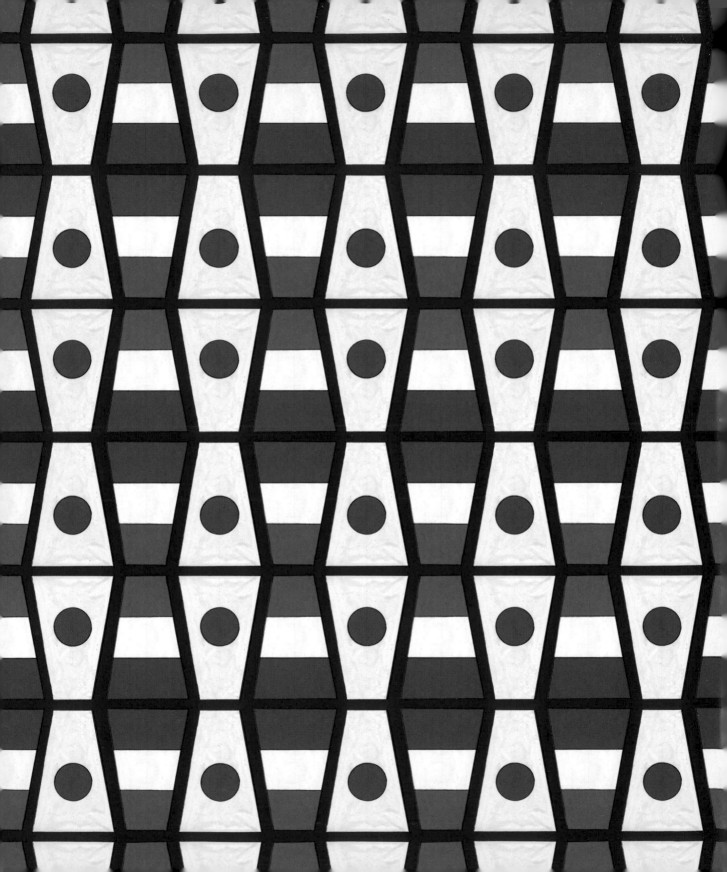

ABOUT WHY
I AM, AND ALWAYS
WILL BE, A
DEEP-SEA
DIVER
N.º 13

As I resurface, a ray of sunshine pierces the sky. The waves have stopped dancing. Now the sea is like a flying saucer: flat and smooth. I see Richard and Carlotta hugging each other in the distance. Without thinking, and with my diving suit still on, I start rowing. I row our boat toward theirs, the two forming a pair of almond-shaped eyes.

"Have you been fighting sharks again?" Richard asks before giving me a hug.

"More or less . . ." I laugh as I look at Amedeo Limonta. There are strange wrinkles on his face, creases around his mouth. He's smiling. I've never seen him smile before.

Beautiful things should be shared . . .

. . . and there's nothing more beautiful than our sea.

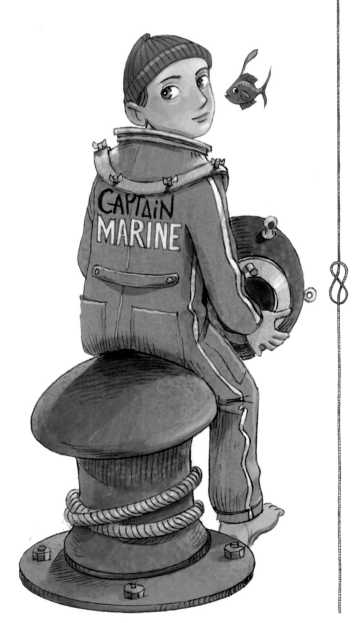

"Hi, Dad!" says Carlotta. "You're not angry?"

"No, not anymore, my most precious little pearl," he says, holding her tight in his arms.

I can't wait to get back home. I want to ask Mom and Dad if we can throw a party at the Marina. Beautiful things should be shared (that's what people say around here), and there's nothing more beautiful than our sea.

We're so far from land that I feel like I've always lived out here, in the middle of nothing. Or in the middle of everything. It depends on how you look at things.

There was one thing I was now sure of. It was completely clear. When I got home, I was going to phone the reporter and tell him that my future had been written today, in the middle of this blue sea: I am, and always will be, a deep-sea diver.

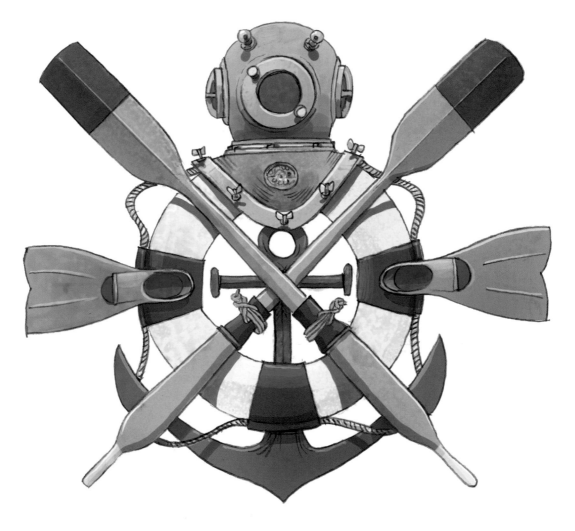

Before I end this story, I should describe to you where everything happened.

We live in a small but ancient village where one day time decided to stop for a cup of tea and never got started again. Everything else seems to have stopped as well. But it's not so much that everything's still, as much as it is at peace. The people aren't petrified like stones. It's just that they move gently, almost in step with the wind, which is usually gentle and warm and gives you a lovely push along as you walk.

If you looked down at our village from a cloud, you'd see that it's a row of houses on a hill covered in smooth grass that, like a flowing gown, spills down into the blue of the sea. Maybe it's the way it's made, with hills on one side and the sea on the other, that's stopped the village from growing: there's nowhere to go up but the sky and going down would mean building on stilts. So, everything is packed into this long strip of land, where the streets are so narrow that not even cars can get by.

You get to Richard's home by going up a hundred thousand steps. It's the highest house in the village, but the view from his garden is so good that as soon as you get to the top, you forget that you're panting and your legs are hurting. It's like the sea is under your feet up there.

A little downhill from Richard's house is the school, which is near the square, where you find the tourist information office and the other offices that grown-ups use. All around the square, like a necklace, are all the shops that you've probably already imagined: a small supermarket, a baker, a clothes shop, and a café with tables outside.

But the stalls that the men and women set up in the morning and take down at night are much better. They sell all kinds of things, like flip-flops, wicker chairs in every size, little wooden boats, fishing rods and tackle, red and blue plates and bowls, and linen curtains that flap in people's faces as they go by.

The vendors have distinctive faces, with big bushy eyebrows and fogged-up, half-broken glasses. But they have kind hearts and happy bellies, and when they talk to each other, they swap secrets and lunch recipes.

If you turn left at the square, there's a grove of umbrella pine trees. In the evening, it's filled with stars and owls (as well as the tree houses that kids have built there). In the spring, the grass turns red and blue with poppies and primroses. Squirrels and mice make their houses in the trees.

But the most beautiful part is after the forest. Once you step out from under its canopy, the plants grow low and far apart, tickling your ankles as you walk by. And then you see the sea, laid out in front of you like an infinite blue sheet.

Then there's a path that takes you down to the beach between stone walls covered with caper plants with pink and white flowers. The path isn't straight, though: it branches off to the left and right like an octopus's tentacles. But you don't need to worry about getting lost, because whatever direction you choose, you'll always get to the beach. If you want, as you walk, you can keep your eyes on the Marina, which is on the end of the pier. You'll recognize it because it has a wooden roof and a little tower with a sailboat and lots of colorful flags.

Then you step onto the sand at the bottom. If it's early morning, there'll always be fisherman over by the rocks with buckets full of sea urchins, mussels, or sardines. If it's November, they might even have *mantis* shrimp, a local delicacy. And this is the spot where we all start to feel at home, away from the square and the offices, with our bare feet and short-sleeved shirts. The old men play bocce on the beach, while little children learn to walk and people let their dogs run free.

There's room for everyone here, and we have everything we need: boats, sea, and sun. Our village will never be famous. You'll probably have a hard time even trying to find us. But if you close your eyes and use your imagination, you'll see that it's the most beautiful village there is.

Richard's House

The Beach Store

The Wood

The Bocce Court

The

The Tourist Office

Market

CAFFE

BARDLINO

The School

The Cafe

The Marina

The Lighthouse

THE CREATORS

ELISA SABATINELLI was born in Fano, Italy, in 1985. As a young girl, her family moved to her mother's hometown of Barcelona in Spain. There she attended school and graduated college with a degree in screenwriting. Unsure of what to do next, she got a chance to transfer to London to work in the press office of a small recording company.

After a year, she found work at a television production company in Milan. During this time she attended the Raul Montanari creative writing school and began to submit stories to magazines and literary contests.

In 2013 she created the festival Cortili Letterari, dedicated to Italian authors under 35, which takes place in Fano every year.

She published some stories and then, in 2016, a novel, *On My Skin* (published by Rizzoli). Since 2008, she has been working as an editorial coordinator in publishing, ghostwriting and reading manuscripts.

Elisa lives in Milan with her husband, Andrea, and her two children, Ottavia and Giovanni. This is her first book for children.

IACOPO BRUNO lives and works between Milan (200 kilometers from the sea) and Levanto (2 meters from the sea). He shares a passion for graphic design and typography with his wife Francesca Leoneschi with whom he founded a studio of graphic arts, illustration, and typography called the World of Dot. He studied at the Academy of Fine Arts in Carrara, dedicating himself for many years to painting. His passion for illustration arrived later when he participated in an illustration contest as part of the Bologna Children's Book Fair. He submitted five spreads dedicated to Peter Pan and was chosen a winner. Since then, his work has traveled the world and been featured in volumes from major international publishers. He has illustrated hundreds of book covers and received recognition from prestigious organizations such as the Society of Illustrators in New York, the Cook Prize, and Junior Library Guild. His picture book *Sergeant Reckless*, written by Patricia McCormick (Balzer & Bray/HarperCollins), won the Texas Bluebonnet Award in 2019. When he is not drawing, he takes his boat in search of dolphins and, if the weather is bad, restores paintings and antique furniture in his cellar full of tools and curiosities.

ACKNOWLEDGMENTS

This story was born 10 years ago and started as a tale of two pages long. One of the first to read it was Iacopo Bruno, who sketched a little Hector inside a large diving suit. In the space inside the helmet is the face of little Hector peering out. Iacopo was able to capture the world exactly as I had it in my mind. In that drawing he had captured the entire essence in one single illustration. Then, Massimiliano "Maci" Verdesca convinced me it could be a cartoon and we offered it to a Japanese production company . . . nothing happened.

Like many projects, it sat still and then it seemed about to start so many times. *The Diver*, as we called it, today is now a book and therefore my heartfelt thanks to Solferino for believing in it and supporting us through to publication.

Thank you to Iacopo, a precious master of more than drawing, to whom I am infinitely grateful to have had the opportunity to work. And, to my husband Andrea, with whom I share the passion of future projects when they are still just thoughts I say out loud.

First of all, I thank Elisa Sabatinelli who one day wrote a story that spoke of a diver which was perfect for me to illustrate, Luisa Sacchi who believed in making this book a reality, Giovanna Ferraris who with talent and good humor held the line through everything, the new parent Pietro Piscitelli who is the undisputed master of calligraphy, and finally Francesca who is my compass.